To my darling Kassius and Nanny Freda

Lorraine Carey

For my two little monsters

Illustrated by
Migy Blanco

First published in 2015 by Nosy Crow Ltd, The Crow's Nest,
10a Lant Street, London SE1 1QR
www.nosycrow.com

ISBN 978 0 85763 313 2 (HB)
ISBN 978 0 85763 314 9 (PB)

Nosy Crow and associated logos are trademarks and/or registered trademarks of Nosy Crow Ltd.

A CIP catalogue record for this book is available from the British Library.

Printed in Italy by Imago
Papers used by Nosy Crow are made from wood grown in sustainable forests.

3 5 7 9 8 6 4 2 (HB)
3 5 7 9 8 6 4 2 (PB)

Cinderella's Sister and the BIG BAD WOLF

nosy crow

Here is Cinderella.

Here is her stepmother,

Mrs Ugly.

Here are the Ugly sisters.

One, two and . . .

. . . three.

You already know the two Ugly sisters,

who were horrid, nasty and mean,

but Gertie, their little sister, was . . . nice.

While Cinderella lazed about and did absolutely **nothing**, Gertie watered the pumpkins, took care of the mice and did **all** the housework.

Niceness shone from Gertie's face and her smile was **brighter** than sunshine.

Well, of course,

the Ugly Family despaired.

They were **ashamed.**

They hid little Gertie away,

and they never let her go **anywhere** with them.

Then, one morning, a special invitation arrived . . .

"Oooh, look!"
said Mrs Ugly.
"We're invited to a
Grand Ball at the
palace tonight!"

"A ball?" cried Gertie. "Oh, please can I go?"

"You?" said Mrs Ugly. "Go to the Ball?
Who'd believe that you're an Ugly sister?
You don't walk Ugly, you don't talk Ugly,
and with that shocking smile on your face,
you don't even look Ugly!"

"But I am an Ugly sister," Gertie begged,
"and I can be bad – I know I can!"

"Well, OK," said Mrs Ugly,
"but you'll need lessons.
A visit to the Wicked Queen
should do the trick!"

So, that afternoon,
Gertie was sent to
the Wicked Queen,
who was just about to visit
Snow White . . . with a poisoned apple.

The Wicked Queen dressed up as a little old lady.

"Hello, my dear," she said to Snow White.

"Won't you take a bite of this **lovely** apple?"

But Gertie couldn't bear to watch.

"Look out, Snow White!" she shouted.

"That's the Wicked Queen –
and that apple is poisoned!"

"No thanks, then,"
said Snow White.

And she shut the door.

Well, the Wicked Queen was furious
and she sent Gertie home, faster than a streak of lightning.
Back at home, Mrs Ugly was very angry, but Gertie begged
for another chance to be mean and bad. "Oh, all right!" said Mrs Ugly.
"But this time you're going to see the Worst Witch of all . . ."

"Being bad is easy,"
said the Worst Witch.
"Let me show you how.
Hansel! Gretel!
Come in, children!

The oven's nice and hot
and I'm planning a **delicious** dinner!"

Gertie tried hard to be bad, **really** she did.

But she just couldn't keep quiet.

"Don't come in!" she blurted.

"That delicious dinner is

YOU!"

"Oh, in that case, we'll be off,"

said Hansel and Gretel.

"We'll just take some snacks with us."

By teatime,

Gertie was back home again,

but now Mrs Ugly was furious.

"Oh, please!" Gertie wailed. "Please let me go to the Ball!

I can be mean and bad, I know I can!"

And she cried so much that in the end Mrs Ugly

agreed to give her one last chance. But this time,

Gertie was sent to the meanest and nastiest baddie of all . . .

. . . the Wolf!

And the Wolf was wearing a frock!

"So, you wanna be Ugly, huh?"

said the Wolf.

"You wanna be BAD?"

"Oh, I do!" said Gertie.
"I do! I do!"

"Well," said the Wolf,
"you're just in time! Watch this!"

Suddenly,
there was a
knock, knock, knock on the door.

And Little Red Riding Hood skipped in.

"Oh, Grandma . . ." said Little Red Riding Hood,
"what big eyes you've got . . ."

"All the better to see you with," said the Wolf.

"Oh, Grandma . . ." said Little Red Riding Hood,
"what big ears you've got . . ."

"All the better to hear you with," said the Wolf.

"Oh, Grandma . . ." said Little Red Riding Hood,
"what big teeth –"

"Stop!" Gertie shouted.
"That's not your grandma, that's . . ."

. . . the Wolf!"

And Little Red Riding Hood scarpered.

The Wolf turned to Gertie and **drooled.**

"Please don't eat me!" said Gertie.
"I've tried so hard to be mean and bad.
I only wanted to go to the Ball, and –"

"Ball?" said the Wolf.
"Did you just say . . . Ball?
Oh, I have always wanted
to go to a ball!"

"Come on,"
said Gertie.
"Let's see what
we can do."

But by the time Gertie and the Wolf arrived home, Mrs Ugly and the two Ugly sisters had already left for the Ball. All was quiet. "We're too late!" cried Gertie, when who should appear but a beautiful fairy!

"I am your Fairy Godmother!" said the Fairy. She looked at Gertie and the Wolf. "And I expect you two want to go to the Ball, don't you?"

"Stop!" shouted an angry voice. "Step away from that wand RIGHT NOW . . ."

It was Cinderella.
And if anyone had been
mean and bad, it was her.
"What about me?"
she screeched.
"I've been waiting all night
for a Fairy Godmother.
And who is that wolf, in
that ridiculous dress?"

Well, Fairy Godmothers
do not like bad manners.
"How dare you be
so rude!" she said,
and she quickly
turned Cinderella
into a . . .

. . . mouse.

But Gertie and the Wolf went to the Ball in beautiful, new dresses.

And a **lovely** time they had, too.

So lovely, in fact, that Gertie and Prince Charming

fell in love and married soon after.

As for Mrs Ugly, and Gertie's
two Ugly sisters . . .

well, no one quite knows

why, but they were never, ever . . .

JUST MARRIED

. . . seen again.